D0468457

Dog Days of School

For Nick and Whimsy
Love, Mom
—K.D.

For Greg
—B.B.

First Edition

10 9 8 7 6 5 4 3 2 1

H106-9333-5-14060

Printed in Malaysia

Library of Congress Cataloging-in-Publication Data

DiPucchio, Kelly S.
Dog days of school / by Kelly DiPucchio ; illustrated by Brian Biggs. — First edition.
pages cm
Summary: Tired of school, Charlie envies his dog and wishes he could be a dog, too, but when his wish comes true he discovers that his life was not all bad.
ISBN-13: 978-0-7868-5493-6
ISBN-10: 0-7868-5493-6
[1. Wishes—Fiction. 2. Dogs—Fiction. 3. Humorous stories.] I. Biggs, Brian, illustrator. II. Title.
PZ7.D6219Dog 2014
[E]—dc23 2013021227

Reinforced binding

Visit www.disneyhyperionbooks.com

Dog Days of School

By Kelly DiPucchio

Illustrated by Brian Biggs

Disney • HYPERION BOOKS
New York

Charlie did not like going to school.

He was tired of practicing his letters.
He was tired of drawing pictures.
He was tired of trying to explain himself
to the teacher.

Charlie was even tired of being tired.

Sunday nights were always hard for Charlie. His stomach did flip-flops, and he could not fall asleep.

“You’re lucky you don’t have to go to school,” Charlie told Norman.

Norman rolled over on his back and snored.

Charlie looked out the window and found the brightest star in the sky.

"I wish I was a dog," Charlie sighed.

On Monday morning, Charlie woke up on the floor. He scratched his ear with his right foot and yawned. Charlie's mother came into the room and patted Norman's head.

"It's time to get up for school, sleepyhead," she said.

Norman jumped down
from Charlie's bed.

He ate breakfast.

He brushed his teeth,

and then he hurried out
the door to catch the bus.

Charlie smiled. He rolled over
on his back and snored.
Ahhh . . .

At school, Norman took Charlie's seat at Table Two. The children gave Norman a curious look and went back to practicing their letters.

Norman practiced his letters, too.

Back at home, Charlie looked out the window and watched the leaves fall—

for hours . . .

and hours . . .

and hours.

On Tuesday,
Norman went to school
and made a clay sculpture,

and a food pyramid.

He ate birthday cupcakes
and took a long, cold drink
from the water fountain.

Charlie ate dry biscuits
and took a long, cold drink...

...from the toilet.

On Wednesday, Norman learned
how to play house,
and kickball,
and the maracas.

Charlie learned how to play fetch . . .

. . . and how not to!

On Thursday, Norman
built a house out of
blocks,

painted a
self-portrait,

and went on a field trip.

Charlie went on a field trip, too.

On Friday, Norman
ran into some trouble
with the scissors
and the glue.

The teacher scolded him
for chewing on his pencil,

and the table,

and her shoes.

And he had to sit
through a long,
awful, boring story
about a cat.

Across town, Charlie had to sit through a long, awful, boring day at the dog groomer's.

The weekend wasn't much better.

Norman tried to play soccer.

He tried to sit through a movie.

And he tried to finish a triple hot-fudge banana sundae with extra whipped cream.

Meanwhile,

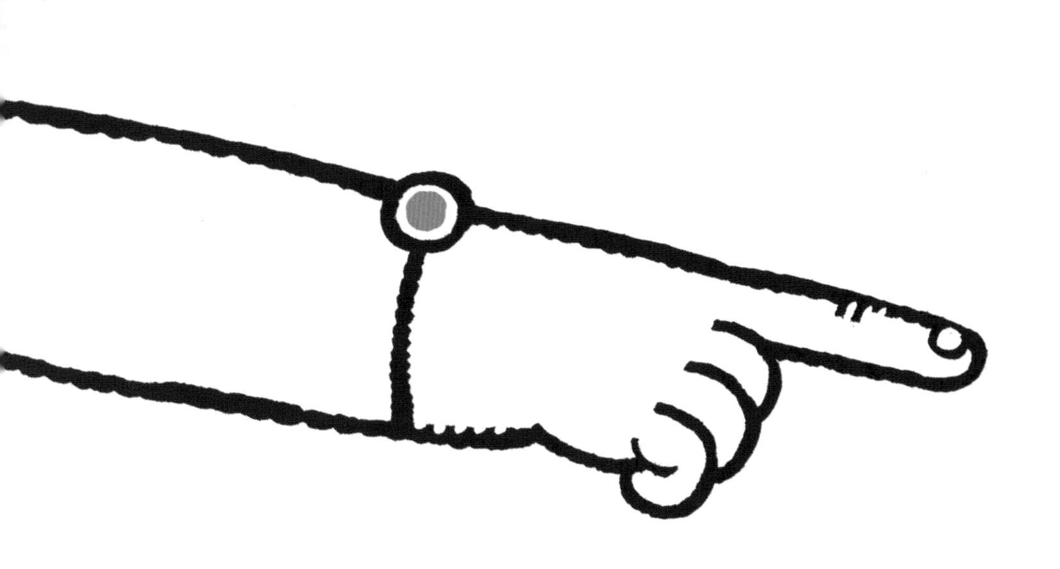

Charlie spent his weekend
locked up in the laundry room.

By Sunday evening,
Charlie had had enough.

He tried to write
his parents a note.
(But they couldn't read it.)

He tried to draw
them a picture.
(But it wasn't very good.)

He tried explaining to them,
"I'M NOT NORMAN!"
(But his parents only heard,
WOOF! WOOF! WOOF!)

"Bad dog!" said
Charlie's mother.
And she put him
outside in the cold.

The wind howled, and Charlie shivered.
Creepy shadows danced across the lawn.
Charlie's stomach did flip-flops, and
he could not fall asleep.
He looked up at the stars and sniffed,
"I really wish I was a boy again!"

On Monday morning, Charlie woke up in his own bed. His mother came into the room and kissed his forehead. "Time to get up for school, Charlie," she said.

Charlie jumped out of bed.

He got dressed.

He ate breakfast.

He brushed his teeth.

Charlie went to school.

And Norman?

Norman took
a very,
very
long nap.